NOT SO PERFECT

STORIES

BY NIK PERRING

Roastbooks

This paperback edition first published in 2010 by
Roastbooks Ltd.
www.roastbooks.co.uk

A catalogue record of this book is available from the British Library

ISBN: 978-1-906894-07-8

Illustrations: Roastbooks ltd
Cover design: Luke Best
Photo: Hannah Young

Praise for *Not So Perfect*

These short short stories are glorious ammunition to fire at those who link brevity with insubstantiality.
Tania Hershman, author of *The White Road and Other Stories*.

An unforgettable assortment of wonky connections that glitter with truthfulness, that spill out ache, that make me nod my head and whisper, yes.
Caroline Smailes, author of *Like Bees to Honey*.

This marvellous collection resonates with a surreal impishness, exploring with a wry smile the often unfathomable complexities that underpin our relationships. He offers no answers, but demands that we look again. And again. In so doing he greatly enriches those who read him.
Vanessa Gebbie, author of *Words From a Glass Bubble*.

Nik Perring's moving and imaginative flash fictions capture whole lives in just a glimpse, a character, a snatch of dialogue, and a few perfectly chosen details. These short, short stories are so full of life.
Michael Kimball, author of *Dear Everybody*.

Don't be fooled by the title, this collection of stories rubs shoulders with perfect storytelling on numerous occasions.
Joe Melia, coordinator of the The Bristol Short Story Prize.

For Ken, Annie and Marion.

Kiss - page 9

Bare and Naked in Siberia - page 15

When You're Frightened, Honey, Think of Strawberries - page 21

Shark Boy - page 25

Not Nitro - page 31

My Wife Threw Up a Lemur - page 35

Seconds Are Ticking By - page 41

Pacifier - page 45

The Mechanical Woman - page 49

Watching, Listening - page 53

Lump - page 59

My Heart's in a Box - page 65

Two Old Women Birdwatching in My Garden - page 73

The Other Mr Panossian - page 77

Pieces of Us - page 83

Say My Name - page 87

In my Head I'm Venus - page 93

Where Did He Go, You Wonder - page 99

Sobs - page 105

The Angel in The Car Park - page 113

Number 14 - page 117

Five Years and The Last Night on Earth - page 127

Kiss

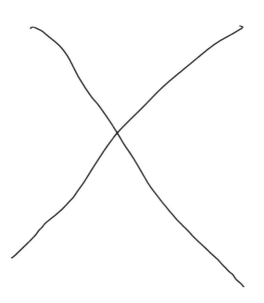

The man was rude to his wife, mostly. But she loved him all the same, loved him as much as when they'd met – her, fresh out of college, him with flecks of grey already creeping into his hair. Decades on, she was still young, black haired, funny, smart. And she was good at her job, well liked by those she managed, and she earned a good wage. Still, when she came home he'd often ignore her, or choose to grunt instead of speaking.

She loved to cook, and she loved to cook for him – and she was good at it, and not just at your average meal. Her teriyaki was as good as her hot pot and her madras was as good as anything. But mostly, despite cleaning his plate, he'd be rude, critical, grumpy.

'It's fine,' he'd snap if she pushed him for a verdict on something new or recently perfected.

He was retired, had been for years, and his days were predictable, but she still asked him about them.

'How was your day?' she'd say, a warm smile on soft lips.

'Fine.'

She'd ask, 'Been in the garden? How are the plants?'

Sometimes, if he was in the right mood, he'd tell her what he'd been doing, tell her what he planned to do, use words like compost, borders,

11

trimming, pruning, and colour.

He loved his garden, and not just because he enjoyed the work, or because he appreciated the exercise and fresh air, or because he loved its smells and colours. He and his plants were friends. He'd talk to them, tell them secrets. Give them instructions – explain when to bloom, and for how long, show them why they should adjust the angles of their stems, which way they ought to face. And the plants listened. But this was a secret. No-one could know.

The man's wife knew. Not that she said anything, if it made him happy then fine.

She'd seen him a number of times, watched him from their kitchen window, seen him with his head inclined towards a hanging basket, nodding as he spoke to it, or with his hands on his hips, chatting to their cherry tree. One day she'd come home to find him on his knees, arms waving, conducting their bedding plants.

The first time she mentioned it to him was on the day he died.

He'd become grey and thin very quickly; he had begun to look like an old man, and she, his wife, was worried.

She found him in their room. He was cupping the head of a poinsettia, whispering to it tenderly and with enthusiasm. She heard him tell it her name.

'Hi,' she said, 'How are you doing?'

'Fine,' he said.

'Is it true what they say?' she asked, easing herself onto their bed, 'Does it help them grow?'

'Some people think so,' he told her.

'What do you say to them?' asked his wife, patting their mattress, inviting him to join her.

He straightened and smiled. The mattress creaked under his weight.

'Ever think what you'll do when I'm gone?' he asked.

'Don't be silly! There's life in you yet,' she said, that warmth on her lips, hoping.

'I think about it,' he continued. 'You'll be a long time without me.'

'Don't talk like that.'

'Wish I was younger,' he said. 'Or that you were older. Big gap between us.'

The man's wife hushed him. She didn't want to hear this.

'So the flowers,' she said. 'What do you tell them?'

'Secrets,' he said. 'Instructions. Things they need to remember once I've gone. And they will, you know,' he told her, smiling, 'Just you wait.'

She pulled him close and held him, because she loved him. They lay together that night, old next to young, man next to wife. He told her he loved her and that he always would – and that she should believe what he said about the flowers – and he apologised for being grumpy most of the time and explained that it was because he felt guilty for being so much older – and he said that he thought he was selfish and she told him to sshhh.

In the morning he was dead, died in his sleep.

With a funeral to arrange and friends and relatives to deal with and wills to action – and everything else that comes with losing a husband – the woman, now a widow, didn't think about the flowers or about what her husband had said. She went weeks once without watering them.

She was in the garden when it came back to her, she was just there, just breathing, when she noticed that the flowerbed was different – its flowers made shapes. Letters. Words.

The words spelled her name, they spelled ALWAYS and, at the end, after the blues and yellows and pinks that formed the name of her husband, they made an X.

Bare and Naked in Siberia

They found a woolly mammoth in the ice. It was on the TV. I saw it. It was a baby called Lyuba and it wasn't woolly at all. It was bare, naked. It was a hot day so I'd put ice in my lemonade; ice was where they'd pulled Lyuba from, where she'd been for thousands of years. I thought about Eskimos and polar bears and their heavy furs and then about penguins with their insulation; and there was Lyuba, bare and naked in Siberia. She'd have been so cold, I thought.

Dad was enthralled, engrossed. His back was arched as he sat in his chair and I'd not seen him that interested in anything since they'd announced the credit crunch. He'd sat there, night after night after night, stooping towards the TV, watching the news or some financial programme like he was a lion stalking it. Or maybe, I thought, maybe he was a buffalo, watching out for lions.

The credit crunch affected me. Things in my life changed, they stopped, got lost, disappeared.

First to go were the soaps on the TV. One day Dad came into the living room. He looked out of place, kind of flustered like how I used to get before concerts with orchestra when I was younger. He picked up the remote and thumbed one of its buttons, switched from Hollyoaks to the news. He sat in his chair and watched two men in suits sitting at a desk, talking and shaking their heads. There were graphs and numbers and lots of percentage signs.

Dad said, 'Shush, Olivia. This is important,' and then, 'You don't need the TV to do your homework. Just get on with it, eh?'

So I did. Me, on my front on the carpet, with my books and pens and folders, white iPod earphones in my ears, doing my revision, and Dad in his chair, straining towards the telly. This went on for months. Usually he wouldn't even take off his jacket or loosen his tie. He looked like he was concentrating so hard: shoulders up, chin forward – we both were – and that's where he'd stay, barely altering his position, until Mum called through from the kitchen to tell us that dinner was ready.

Dinnertime changed too, but I didn't really mind; it became a one-course affair. No pudding, no afters. No donuts or arctic roll or Cherry Bakewells. I think Dad missed them the most. He didn't complain though, didn't mention it. When he'd finished he'd get up and clear away our plates, just like before, and then he'd boil the kettle to make tea; he and Mum had taken to sharing a bag.

One day Dad came home early. He was carrying a plastic bag from the off licence. There was a bottle of wine in it and Mum looked so scared when he pulled it out. He told her not to worry and gave her a great big bar of Dairy Milk. I got a bag of Revels. They drank the wine at dinner and talked about The Redundancies.

'Last ones in, first ones out,' Dad said. 'Cheers.' Glasses clinked.

'I am so relieved,' Mum said, and she said that if I wanted, I could have a glass. I said no because I had an exam in the morning.

Even though, financially, we'd be okay – Dad had been told his job was safe, secure – we didn't go back to having afters. The Cherry Bakewells didn't find their way back onto Mum's shopping list, and the soaps didn't find their way back onto the TV.

That was when I started doing my bit. Just in case. I started to save the money Mum gave me for lunch. I put it in an old shoe box every night when I got home. That was part of the routine: say Hi to Mum, run upstairs to dump my bag and get changed. Shoes in the cupboard with the box of money; shirt and tights in the washing basket; and skirt and blazer hung on wire hangers.

I'd stand in front of the mirror and turn slowly in my underwear, watching myself, looking at the progress.

I lost loads of weight, which was good because Paul Hart said that he liked girls who were skinny and Paul Hart was a good kisser. He said he liked that my tits were small, he told me that when he was touching them, which felt quite nice. He told me another time, when his hand was up my skirt, that he wanted to shag me – Can I? – and I said I'd like that, and I wondered where we could do it and whether I'd enjoy it and if I'd be any good. Some girls had had shags and they'd said that it was fucking amazing but I'd heard it could hurt a bit. And I'd had Paul Hart's dick in my hand a few times and it had felt big and I was worried.

'I'd really like to,' I told him and he kind of groaned and said, 'How about now?' and I'd gone all flushed and dizzy and shaky, and I wished I'd had lunch, and I said, 'Okay' and I followed him deeper into the bushes in the park and I clenched my fists as he pulled down his trousers and grinned at me wildly.

I finished my lemonade and continued watching Dad watching the programme about the woolly mammoth they'd found in Siberia. I thought of Lyuba. I thought of her in the ground, in the ice, thought she must have been so cold, so weak, with no fur, all bare like that. And I thought: I know exactly how that feels. Poor thing.

When You're Frightened, Honey, Think of Strawberries

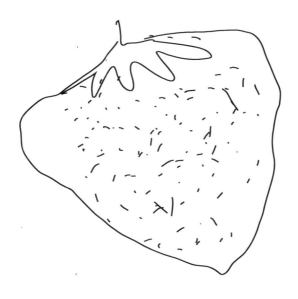

She remembers now what she was told when she was small: When you're frightened, Honey, think of strawberries.

So she does. She's been thinking about them ever since he started talking. While his words bite her she thinks of their spidery tops. She thinks of strawberries as he explains, justifies, tells her why this isn't working, why this must end. Strawberries: she thinks of all the shades they could be; as pink as her lips or deep, dark, like the blood when he cut his finger dicing onions yesterday. The red of his wound soothes her.

Strawberries she thinks, as he unlatches the door, and she remembers how cold their skins can be. She could think of them in a bowl, cream folded around them, but she doesn't. She'd rather see them on their own; almost heart shaped. She pictures their seeds, like a hundred lonely eyes. And she wishes they had pits so she could spit them at him.

And because all she can think of are strawberries and pits and colours and leaves, she is unable to reply. There is nothing to say.

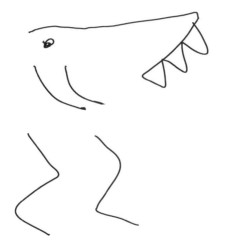

Shark Boy

Shark Boy just couldn't stop. Just couldn't stop. He had to keep doing, had to keep moving or else he'd die; the doctors told his mother this moments after his birth – 'Just like a shark,' they said. And for his mother, a single parent, Shark Boy's early years were difficult and tiring. But if her son, her only family, couldn't stop then she'd do her damndest to be like that too, to share and to understand. The baby books told her that empathising was important. She gave it her all. At night she'd sit in a chair by his bed, always ready to entertain him, to read to him, to watch him walk and walk and walk around his room, or just to tell him stories, and stroke his hair.

◆

As Shark Boy grew he learned how to manage his condition; treated it like it was Tourette's or diabetes. He learned that he could substitute endless talking or walking – walking – walking, for thinking; doing with his mind. And it worked. Shark Boy was exceptionally good at mental arithmetic, at solving equations, and he was just as good at riddles and puzzles. He even won some local competitions and could, his teacher thought, have gone on to do well in the nationals. But Shark Boy refused to compete. He was scared that if he won he'd have less to concentrate on, less to think about. It scared him very much.

◆

Shark Boy became a scientist – a particularly brilliant one. He specialised in Quantum Mechanics and really should have won a Nobel Prize for illustrating how it and Einstein's theory of relativity were connected. He helped people understand Picasso too, which pleased him.

He was in a café when the end came. He'd been working hard, hunched over a notebook, and he was beginning to really understand Black Holes and The Big Bang; there was a closer relationship between them than anyone could have suspected.

A woman was sitting at the table next to him, and boy was she beautiful. When she smiled at him he shrunk into his suit, embarrassed. But his mind switched to the possibilities of love, and sex and companionship. His mind thought about how she'd: look, taste, feel, smell, sound. Shark Boy had thoughts of family, the kids they could have, what they'd be called, how they'd do at school, what they'd grow up into – of how he'd feel when the house was all empty when they left. And he thought of them, him and the woman, as an old couple, thought how he could love her wrinkles, her newness, her changed body.

Shark Boy was in love. He wanted her, wanted this forever. And when she smiled at him a second time his world stood still.

And that's how Shark Boy died.

Not Nitro

There was a girl who could spit fire – long, slim jets of it, more impressive and ten times hotter than anything you'd see from a street performer or at the circus. But her name was Lucy, not Salamander or Flame or Nitro. It was Lucy, simply Lucy.

It came about, the fire-spitting, quite suddenly and it was wholly unexpected.

One minute she was Lucy. Simply Lucy; sweet and plain and pretty, a good and loyal wife, calm inside, and with an interest in pot plants, archaeology and Roman history. Then, she changed.

He was quite honest about it all, and quite clear.

'I'm having an affair,' he said. 'And I don't want to be having an affair any more. I'll take my things now, no need for this to drag on.'

Everything was brought to the boil inside her.

For a moment she said nothing, but she could feel herself bubbling over. She could feel it rising up from her gut, scalding her throat. She felt her jaw shake, her lips judder; it looked like she was shivering.

And then – bam! Her mouth was a volcano and the volcano erupted. A column shot from her mouth and it was red, molten and it burned. Smoke plumed thickly from her nostrils.

He left, singed and smoking, quickly and without his things.

And as he ran for the door Lucy thought of Pompeii and she felt like a mountain.

My Wife Threw Up a Lemur

We were in the middle row on a plane on a flight back from Europe when my wife threw up a lemur. She heaved. Flailed her arms and knocked my glass of ginger ale off the plastic pull-down tray and over me. It pooled in my lap. I thought she was choking on a peanut and I was about call out for a doctor but she puked it up before I could. She threw it up into her hands, caught it. And there it was: a tiny lemur. It sat there, shivering and staring up at us both with its huge round eyes.

The stewardesses were accommodating; they found us some seats near the back where we had more space. They brought the lemur a blanket and a bowl of water, and some paper towels for me, then left us to get on with it.

◆

It was while we were cleaning out our lemur's cage that my wife threw up her second animal: a tortoiseshell kitten. Same big eyes as the lemur and she turned out to be just as friendly, and the two got on wonderfully. They'd play together, groom each other and when the winter came they kept each other warm. We joked, me and my wife, said they were like brother and sister.

◆

Last year we moved out of our apartment and into a house. We needed somewhere with space for fish tanks and birdcages, needed somewhere with room enough for the snake and the gecko. Our friends don't seem bothered about our animals, they don't seem interested to tell you the truth. No-one's ever asked where they've come from. I kind of wish they would.

I play with the animals when my wife's out. I've been trying to train the lemur to do a kind of trapeze thing from the fan on the hall ceiling. I want him to swing down and land on the cat's back. That'd be some party trick. I've something planned for the turtle and the meerkat too but that'll have to wait.

Last week my wife cooked me dinner. A special one. Good cut of pork, expensive vegetables. Fresh sage. Creamy mash.

I knew what was coming. I knew what all this was about. She needn't have gone to any trouble because I'd have said yes. We've always said we'd love kids one day.

It was while we were trying that it happened again. I was just coming to the end, almost coming, when she pushed me off. She was wrenching and heaving and all I could do was watch and pant.

She threw up a rat, small and grey and cuter than I'd imagined rats to be, and she lay there stroking it. The room smelled of sex and sweat and fur.

I said to her, 'We can try again tomorrow.'

And she kind of shrugged, nodded. Then slid out of bed, cradling the rat in her arms, and she went downstairs to find it somewhere to sleep.

tick tock

Seconds Are Ticking By

teck tock
tick tock

So what would you do in my situation? Your mate, Mike, has been showing you the grenade he found amongst his granddad's belongings. You're holding it. It's cold. Interesting. Alien. And you've just, by complete mistake, pulled out the pin.

You're off the school bus, that pulled away five minutes ago, and you're ten minutes walk from home. There are fields on either side of the road. You can't just toss it and run, can you?

Actually, you can. You have to. You've pulled the pin out! You have no idea how long it'll be before it explodes – if it explodes at all – but you know you can't have much time. Mike knows that as well. That's why he's pelting, up the hill, away from you.

You run to the fence. You toss the grenade as far as you can. You're happy with the distance you get, pretty much, though you'll have to make a run for it to be sure you'll be safe.

You're relieved. But only for a second. The panic returns. You feel it in your belly, in your legs. Your eyes are wide.

It's landed near the farmer.

Seconds are ticking by.

You need to get away from it. Away from the danger.

You need to warn the farmer.

This could be murder.

You shout. You scream warnings at him. Scream so loudly your throat burns.

But he's keeping his back to you. Hasn't heard.

And the seconds are ticking by.

You will try one last time. You have to. But you have to get away too. You don't want to be responsible for killing or maiming someone, but you need to protect yourself. It's human nature.

Again you scream.

Still he stays rigid. Deaf to you.

And then: a moment of clarity.

You panic.

You realise.

This is not the farmer.

This is a scarecrow.

And seconds are ticking by.

Pacifier

Their argument is fuelled by heat and humidity. It is fierce. The air conditioning packed in before lunch and now, even though it's almost evening, the atmosphere's sticky and heavy and hot.

The bald man is sitting on the bed, shirt unbuttoned down to his navel. He has dark patches under his arms.

He says to his wife, who's standing next to the open window, he says, 'No.' And she says, for what feels like the thousandth time, 'Why not? You –' she says, 'It's always about you. Always about what you want.'

He says, 'Bah! But you know it's a stupid idea. Fucking stupid, as fucking stupid as you. Never work. Waste of time. Waste of money.'

And when she's sick of saying please, sick of his refusal to see sense, to see where his wife's coming from, she tells him that he can go to hell.

The heat and humidity fuel their anger.

The man, dry-mouthed, bald, sweating and uncomfortable, reminds her of her past. The time she did fucking this, the time she did fucking that, forgot this, let him down that way.

She responds by reminding him.

'Remember? Not so perfect yourself, eh!'

And then something changes. In an instant. He sees her breast – it's the way she's standing – instead of a hidden shadow, he sees shape, skin, a nipple. And she can feel, somehow, the change in him.

Staring, her jaw set and lips pressed together, she hitches up her dress.

And for a moment there is silence.

The Mechanical Woman

She ticked when she moved and she thought that no man could ever love her. When she moved she sounded like clockwork and under her skirt were cogs and wheels, gears and shafts.

A man, she knew, would want to lift up her skirt and see flesh, see pink. Taste skin not oil. A man would want warmth not metal.

She was on a train. She had ticked and clicked down the aisle and found a seat.

The man who sat next to her was on his way home from a convention. He was an enthusiast, he said, an engineer. He worked on models. He loved making things, fixing them, he told her. Anything that could be tightened or tweaked, anything that could be oiled, and anything that could be worked on with a screwdriver or spanner or wrench – well, he said, they were for him.

'You really do love all those things, don't you?' said the woman.

And he said, 'Oh yes. I like to see how things work. Like to see them working as they should.'

'But what if the mechanism's old?' she asked. 'What if it's been neglected?'

'Then it can be cleaned. Polished.'

51

'Could you work on something you'd never seen before?' she asked him.

'That,' he said, 'would be a joy.'

She looked down at her long skirt for a moment, and then met his eye. Smiled. She said, 'I think I have something I'd like to show you.'

1.

At first the librarian smiles at him, even gives him a nod, as the doors slide open and let him in. Once he's past her, her smile sours. She watches him carry out his usual routine, watches him while she rummages through the day's delivery, hoping that someone's taken her advice of what to order, of what to read next. She fingers the spines of three Mr Men books, hard and soft at the same time, and watches.

2.

He knows his routine. He's been doing it for months, but he's not yet comfortable with it. He doesn't like how it makes him feel, it's like he's some kind of thief.

First it's an interested glance at the Just Returned shelves. He might pull out a couple, turn them around, read their blurbs; maybe open one and read a paragraph or two before shaking his head slightly and pushing them back. After hovering briefly by Fiction it's on to DIY, for a more considered look.

He pulls out a book on woodwork, turns its pages. That'll do, he thinks so he tucks it under his arm. He moves over to Self-Help then, not because he thinks he needs it but because it offers him the best view. For some reason there are not many books on that shelf and the ones that are on it are stood up, showing their covers. There are windows to look through.

He's tense, but when he sees her he breathes out, too loudly perhaps. He's relieved: she's here. She's already hoisted the child onto her knee and she is about to begin.

He sits on the lone seat, the low one with its back against the wall. Between him and her – between him and the low settee she's sitting on, and the colourful picture book stand in front of it – is a shelf. The shelf with few books on. The shelf with windows.

He opens his book, the one about woodwork, and pretends to read, but out of the corner of his eye, through the window of books, he watches.

3.

The librarian watches too. She's disappointed because not one person has ordered anything that she's suggested this week. It annoys her. She reads all

56

the book blogs, reads The Bookseller online: she knows what's hot. But her advice falls on deaf ears, no-one listens to what she has to say.

She doesn't like what she sees. Doesn't like him. He does this every week, times his visit so it coincides with that woman's. The librarian is suspicious, this whole thing makes her feel slightly sick, but she can't do anything about it because, officially, he's done nothing wrong. He just sits there, in his anorak and jeans, pretending to mind his own business. She watches, waiting for him to make a move. If only he would.

The woman has her daughter on her knee. The picture book is open. The mother points and makes shapes with her mouth that her daughter – still wrapped up against the cold in a puffed pink coat and fluffy shoes – mimics, almost getting it right.

4.

He doesn't think the woman with the child has noticed him, he hopes she hasn't.

It's the librarian he worries about. He thinks she watches him, doesn't think she trusts him. But once the mother begins he forgets all of that.

'One. Two,' she says. Delicate. Slowly. Her tone is sweet and calm. 'Choo-choo.' It's as though there's no-one more important in the whole world.

'Three. Four.'

He closes his eyes. At first he used to remember being all tucked up in his bed – his mother, with her smell and her warmth, next to him, reading; his eyes closed, dancing to her words.

'Driver says: All Aboard!'

He smiles. He's not thinking of his mother now. He's simply enjoying the story, the tone, her voice. Enjoying being read to. He lowers his book, the one on woodwork.

'Five. Six.'

He hopes she'll never stop. His smile is a grin.

And the librarian watches sourly.

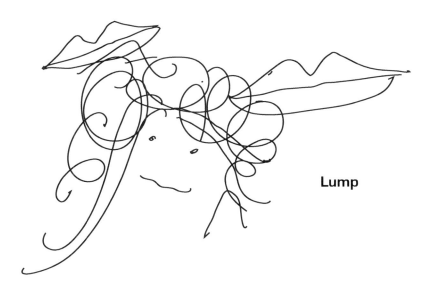

Lump

It was our first date and he found a lump on my breast. It was our first date so we hadn't even kissed yet and, to be honest, I was surprised when I heard myself agreeing to go back to his flat. But I wanted him. Even though I'm not that kind of girl, I wanted him.

It's hard to explain why exactly, but everything seemed right. And I'm not talking about his choice of restaurant (Japanese) or that he'd made me feel brave enough to try sushi, or even the way the wine he ordered went so well with what we were eating – it was him, everything about him seemed to fit.

◆

So, I'm back at his flat. He's taken my coat and hung it behind the door. I'm getting comfortable on the sofa and he's sorting out the drinks. He steps into the room smiling, and he hands me a fat belly of a glass of red. I sip it and it's good and he sits next to me – close – and we talk and talk and talk and my hand finds his. It feels like I'm on the edge of a cliff and about to fall into something wonderful. He kisses me then and it feels that all is well in the world.

I kiss his ear and I like his hand on my stomach and I like his fingers through my hair, they run through it like a waterfall from my neck and down, slowly, slowly, down my back.

When he continues to unbutton his shirt (I've started him on his way) I stand and I wriggle out of my dress and the way he looks at me makes me feel wanted and powerful.

I kick off my shoes and then I'm on top of him and I put my lips, softly, softly, to his neck and he reaches around and undoes the clasp and takes off my bra. He pushes his mouth against mine, I taste his tongue, and he puts a hand to a breast and this all feels so right and everything he does, every movement we make, feels perfectly measured.

And then he stops, his whole body tightens – I can feel it – and he closes his mouth. I probe, try to push my tongue inside but his lips are pressed together and I realise that nothing's going to get through.

It's then that I notice how cold it is in here. Draughty. And I think he must have found something, seen something, smelled or tasted something he can't stand – that's put him off, that's made me ugly. I want to know what it is but I can't bring myself to ask or even look at him because I think I might cry.

That's when he tells me. He's serious and gentle, less tight, and he says I think I felt a lump.

He guides my fingers to it and I can feel it – it's there, this lump, and I am so relieved.

◆

We made love. Up in his room, under his duvet where it's warm. He was so gentle to start with; I think we both forgot about what we'd found.

He asked me about it when we'd finished and I told him that I didn't want to talk about it, but thanks. It would be a shame to ruin something that felt so good, and I liked how he stroked my hair, how it felt like a waterfall, running slowly, slowly, down my back.

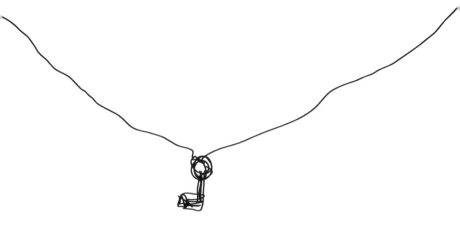

My Heart's in a Box

She kept me awake through the procedure. Awake and anaesthetised. I was in her kitchen, naked and lying on the table.

'It won't hurt, my love,' she whispered and I couldn't feel her kissing my lips. I couldn't feel her slice down my chest or split open my ribcage either. She worked quickly and was done in no time. I saw her pull off her bloodied gloves with a snap and throw them in the sink.

She only let me see it once she'd stitched me up. She cut the thread, dropped the needle in the bin and then took my hands and pulled me upright, helped me off the table and to my feet.

I gasped.

'It's beautiful,' I said and it was: my heart, red and fresh and beating, inside a small box, black on the outside, and lined with purple velvet. She closed the lid and locked it. A silver chain was threaded through the key and she hung it around her neck.

◆

I healed quickly – but, as she said, it hadn't been the usual sort of operation. I didn't need drugs to help with my recovery, she explained, because I had love, because I had her.

Before the procedure I'd been nervous.

I'd said to my lover, 'I'll gladly give you my heart, but are you sure I won't need it?'

She'd said, 'Love doesn't only make the world go round,' so I left it. I think we made love then. It was all going to be fine.

◆

At first she kept the box that contained my heart in the kitchen, on display. We spent a lot of time there so it made sense – that way we'd see it often. It was a kind of solid celebration of what we had and of all there was to come.

One day she moved it, put it on the mantle in the living room. Next to the clock her mother had given us.

She'd asked, 'You don't mind, do you?' and I'd told her, 'Of course not.' I'd said, 'If you're happy then I'm happy.' She gave me a smile then, said, 'How does it look?'

'Great,' I told her. 'Just right.'

◆

The box has been moved around a few times since. It's been in the bathroom and the hall. Spent time on the landing and in our bedroom.

Today I found it in the garage. We're having a clean-out. My lover is sorting through the drawers in the kitchen, she's throwing out old take away menus and fliers for restaurants, binning snapped rubber bands and inkless biros. My task is the garage. I'm sorting through clutter, separating junk from the stuff that's worth keeping.

The box my heart's in is on the windowsill, with the slug pellets and matches, with the almost full bottle of turps and a dusty bottle of champagne we won somewhere.

I put down my brush and I take hold of the box. It's light. For the first time in years I want to open it. I'm curious to see how it looks, wondering if it's as red and as fresh as when I gave it away. I can't of course; the box is locked.

And that starts me thinking: I can't remember the last time I saw my lover with its key on the chain around her neck; she took it off last Christmas so she could wear the pearls I bought her. I don't know if I've seen it since.

I love my lover. I do. But I do wonder about things. I wonder what would happen if we split up. Wonder if she'd lie me on the kitchen table again, anaesthetise me, cut me open neatly and put it back. Or whether I'd be kicked out and the box tossed in with the rubbish.

And I have that image in my mind, of the black box with my heart in it, thrown into a plastic bin bag, sinking in the vegetable peel and empty packets. Drowning. And that image is in my head, it's as strong as the smell of the dust I've freed with my sweeping, when my lover steps through the door. She has a cup of tea in her hand for me. She puts it on the table we use in the garden when it's sunny, and then she puts her arms around me and pulls our bodies together.

She's hugging me, and it's warm and it feels like she means it so I guess I should take that as a sign that everything is going to be all right. But when it stops...

I don't know how I'll feel when it stops.

I hold her tighter. I can smell her hair, I catch some of it in my mouth. And I see the box on the windowsill, with the turps and the matches – it's on its own – and that's when it hits me.

That's when I wonder.

That's when I think: why did I not ask her for hers?

Two Old Women Birdwatching in my Garden

I'd been pretty down since Jo left me. I'd concentrated on work, as you do, to take my mind of it all and my evenings had become pretty similar; I'd slouch on the sofa in the clothes I'd worn to the office, with a beer in my hand, and watch TV programmes I didn't really like. I was aware that I was a cliché.

Last night I heard voices – they were right outside my window, talking. I put down my beer, forced myself to my feet, pulled on my boots and went outside.

I saw two old women, their hair in nets and their bodies covered by long, beige coats.

'What's going on?' I asked.

One turned. 'We're birdwatching.'

'In my garden?' I said. 'At night?'

'It's where the bird is,' she told me. 'We think it might have a nest in that tree.'

She pointed.

I said, 'What kind of bird?' and she told me, but I can't remember its name now, I'm no expert. She seemed pretty excited though, I could see it in her face, so I guess it must have been rare or special.

I sat with them, our three backs against the bricks of my house. And I looked up at the tree. I couldn't see the bird, but I gasped with them and I nodded when they nodded, and I think I ended up being every bit as excited as they were.

If they come over tonight I think I'll make cocoa.

The Other Mr Panossian

Mr Panossian is a friend of mine. He owns Panossian and Sons' General Store on the other side of town; I think it's been there forever. He's a friend of Dad's as well, and Dad makes sure we get all our groceries from him. And now I'm old enough, it's my job to collect them. Dad says it does a boy good to walk over there on a Saturday, that it's good to get some fresh air in my lungs. He says that carrying the grocery bags home, which are neatly filled with eggs, meat, cheese and milk – normal stuff that people eat – as well as whiskey for Dad with two bottles of mixer – that it's good for my arms, that it'll make them strong. He tells me that when I get back, as he ruffles my hair, while Mum fixes me a drink of water.

Every time I push open Mr Panossian's door he smiles at me from behind his counter, asks how I am, says, 'And how is your mother? I hope you're being a good son and that you're looking after her.' And when I tell him, 'Of course,' he says, 'Good man,' and gives me a stick of liquorice.

He says, Man. I like that. It makes me feel as tall as Dad.

Mr Panossian has a brother. Mum talks about him sometimes, though not as often as she used to. He's a traveller, is The Other Mr Panossian. Mum says that I could grow up to be just like him if I'm good and if I eat my vegetables.

She used to like talking about him at the weekends, when Dad was out fishing with the boys.

She'd bring me a sandwich, or a slice of cake, and a glass of lemonade and we'd both sit on the grass in the sun; I'd eat and listen, and she'd talk. She'd talk about all the places The Other Mr Panossian had been (about the time he saw the queen of England, or when he trekked through a jungle, or when he lived on a boat for a year and ate nothing but the fish he caught with the rod he'd made himself) and she'd tell me about all the adventures he'd had; some of them were very funny, but mostly they were exciting.

Often, after she'd gone inside, I'd pretend to be The Other Mr Panossian. I had a branch that a storm had ripped from our tree and I used to pretend that it was his hiking stick; I don't know why I thought The Other Mr Panossian would have a hiking stick – it just made sense to me.

I thought The Other Mr Panossian was the greatest, and I used to wish that he'd come home, take some time off from exploring, to visit his brother at the shop. And I used to hope that while he was in town he'd come and see Mum. Then I could meet him and I could hear all about his adventures and I could ask him what I should do to become an explorer. I hoped he'd bring his stick.

I heard Dad talking to Mum about him once – I think maybe The Other Mr Panossian had sent her a telegram or something. Dad said that he was a coward and a good-for-nothing. He said that running off like that was a disgraceful thing to do, and that he was a bastard for avoiding his responsibilities and leaving some mug to clean up the shit he'd left behind. I never thought Mr Panossian minded working at the shop on his own; he always seemed happy when I saw him.

I asked Mum about it, asked whether The Other Mr Panossian, the explorer, should really be here, whether he should be helping his brother out in the shop. I asked her if he was wrong for leaving him to do all the work while he went off exploring.

Mum said, 'No.' She was very firm about that, and she held me tightly, forcing my chin against her shoulder; I got some of her hair in my mouth. 'No,' she said. But something about it made her so upset she cried.

Pieces of Us

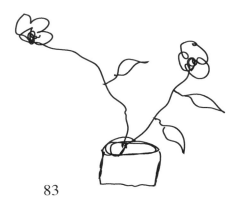

I do this because it makes me feel better. It is a ritual.

I pull out everything that connects me to you: postcards, birthday cards, photos, letters, tickets – a sock, a plant pot. I lay them out in chronological order, set them on the carpet in front of me, and I sit cross-legged and watch. It makes me feel like I'm dying, like I'm seeing our life flash before my eyes. Only, I'm not dying, not really. That's just how it feels.

And though it doesn't seem like it, I am in control; I could scoop everything up and put it back in the Tesco bag whenever I want. But I don't. I leave the pieces of us where they are. They stay there, in their place, on the carpet and I go to bed. I tidy up when my mind's dull in the morning. That's the ritual.

They are laid out now, those pieces of us. Some edges flutter in the breeze.

The ritual ends tonight. I don't know what I'll think come morning.

Tonight, we burn.

Say My Name

He felt as though he was fading, felt as though there soon might not be enough of him to hold the beer he was sipping.

On his own, no-one to distract him, he thought about it – the fading – wondered where it had started.

He remembered an afternoon at school; he was six years old and shy. He remembered how the class had been drawing. Remembered the bell and how they'd moved to put their chairs on the tables and grab their coats, how the teacher had said, 'Excellent work, class,' and clapped her hands three times, as she usually did.

And then she did something different, unexpected. She said, 'I especially liked yours, James.'

It felt as though he'd been pumped full of pride. He beamed.

Then the man remembered another occasion. He remembered standing in a line on the school field, waiting for the captains to pick their teams. He'd been certain it was him being pointed at. He stepped forward but the captain said, 'Not you.' He didn't even use his name. He felt deflated. He felt like gas, like air. Like nothing.

James took another sip of his beer, hoping it wouldn't slip through his skin. It didn't and he smiled. And then his thoughts were of when he'd felt his fullest, the most whole: when he was with Katie.

When she'd said his name it was as though it had weight, as though it had mass, colour. Every time she'd said James, he'd felt that bit bigger, stronger. Anchored. That bit more.

They'd split up a while ago. And he'd been lonely, and chose to stay so, chose not to trouble his friends. That's why he was on his own, here, sipping beer and fading.

Katie, he mouthed, and put down his glass. He tried to remember the last time he'd heard anyone saying his name. But he couldn't. No-one had used his name in months, and he thought: That's why I'm fading.

When he reached for his drink, he could see the table and a beer mat through his arm. He finished it in two clumsy gulps and rushed to the bar.

'Amy,' he said.

'Same again?' she asked.

'Yes,' he said, and then, 'Amy. You know my name, don't you?'

She nodded as she held the glass under the tap's nozzle.

'Say it,' he said.

'Say what?'

'My name. Please, Amy – it's really important.'

'Why?' she asked, watching the beer fizzing in the glass.

'Please, Amy. Just say it.'

She took a breath, flicked off the tap and said, 'Okay. James. It's James.'

But then, when she turned to hand him his drink, she couldn't see him. And in his place was nothing but gas, nothing but air. Nothing.

In My Head I'm Venus

She sees him at the checkout. He's pushing his PIN into the machine and she decides: Yes, I would like a man like that.

She likes how he's standing, likes the lines of his jaw and the shape his hair makes when it meets his neck.

Yes. I would like a man like that, she thinks. And then: yes, I will follow him.

The man is carrying his bag and he's walking towards the exit. She has planned her route. Their paths will converge at the doors.

When she reaches the lingerie section she slows up a little. The man has been caught behind a woman pushing a pushchair and her friend with a trolley.

She can see that he's frustrated. She thinks, if I was with him I'd barge them out of our way. Elbows and shoulders, she thinks. No problem.

The man slips between them. Pardon me. Thank you. Thanks. And then he is able to stride towards the door.

They are on course to meet and in a few moments her life will be changed and his life will be changed and she'll say hello and he'll say hi, and then...

And then. Then it will begin.

She's passed the socks, the wallets and the watches. He's moving away from the jumpers. And here are the doors.

She counts down in her head.

Three.

Two.

One.

GO!

She touches his arm.

He turns. He's surprised.

She says, 'Hello,' and he says 'Hi' and she's not quite sure that she likes his chin.

◆

They are out in the car park. He is surprised and red-cheeked and a little fidgety and she's not sure that she likes his chin.

She introduces herself.

He says, 'And I'm Michael,' and she likes that and she wonders whether a good, strong name can make up for a disappointing chin.

He says, 'I really should be going,' he says it with a smile and she says, 'That's fine,' and she follows him to his car. She stands to one side while he opens the boot and places his bag inside it. She looks into the boot. Thinks: interesting.

He says, 'Well, it's been lovely to meet you,' and yes, she agrees.

Yes it has.

He says, 'But I've got to be somewhere,' so she says, 'Take me with you,' and he looks confused, fidgety again, drums his fingers against his pants, so she explains quickly that she'd better not because her car's here and she'll be needing it. Then she offers him her phone number and he says 'Okay,' and he suggests she leans on his back to write it down.

They touch, through tissue and lipstick and clothes.

From the driver's seat he promises to call and through his window he promises to call. He waves as he pulls away and she waves back, all girly, like a cheerleader, and she blows him a kiss, sends it through his rear window and onto his neck. Mwah.

◆

She's home now. She's been thinking about that chin. Been thinking of cupping it or kissing it, or flicking her tongue against it. She is thinking about being playful. Thinking about taking him and his chin to bed. She is thinking about being playful, and his chin, and her bed – and his name: what a nice shape my mouth makes when I say it. She's thinking about sweat and smells and rocking and him being beneath her and him saying her name and him looking up at her like she's a goddess, like she's a star, like she's Venus.

She's thinking all of these things and the phone is ringing.

It is ringing. Ringing. And she is not answering it.

It is ringing, ringing, and she's not answering it and then it stops.

She does not adjust her position. She stays as she is on the couch, her hands to her chest, and in her head she's Venus.

Where Did He Go, You Wonder

What I want to know is this:

How does it feel?

How does it feel to be walking slowly, stiffly, towards your end?

There was a woman. She was sixty-eight. I want you to put yourself in her place.

Your children are men. They have mortgages far away. They have wives. Your husband is not the man you married. You love him almost as much as you miss him. Often, you wonder where he went. You think this as you watch him dress, wonder where that body, which was never perfect, went. You wonder when it changed shape and wonder how you never noticed. You wonder when he sprouted those hairs, fine and grey, on his shoulders and when the spots on his legs appeared, when he grew that extra skin on his neck and around his nipples.

His smile's the same as you remember (not that you can fully trust your memory now) and sometimes that's a good thing. Sometimes it doesn't leave you feeling hollow.

You wonder where he went as you watch him eat – the food you've prepared for him is healthy, but not because he wants his mind and body sharp, this is to keep the blood flowing through his narrowed arteries, to help his heart that's grown so weak.

Like yours, you think. Weak and heavy. You wonder if your heart has been broken by time, by life, by your husband.

But you play the game. You hold his hand when you stroll slowly through the countryside and when you wander into town on a Sunday for some fresh air and for his papers.

You let him move inside you at night, let him move and shift until he's done. It's all a part of the game. You've not enjoyed it in years. You wish that, even if it's only once in a while, he'd consider doing what you like – he must remember. You wish he'd kiss you where he used to, and how he used to. Where did he go, you wonder.

You ask yourself sometimes if you hate him. And then you wonder if you have the right to think like that – beneath that dye you know your hair's as silver as stars, and you know that he knows that too. You worry that he thinks the same of you – you most often think this while you're in the shower. That's where you shave your legs for him. You wonder whether it's worth the effort, whether he even notices.

From the kitchen window you watch him garden while you scrub potatoes or peel them from their skins. You see him move awkwardly – he's stiff and sore, you know this because you feel it too. He's in his grey trousers and green woolly jumper, you can see his bald patch and his width, and you could cry because he is an old man and you are an old woman and it's right there in front of you. You think of all the things you could have done (and wonder why you never thought of them before) and of all the things you can't do now, and you feel like you could storm out into the garden and strangle him, leave him slumped in the rosebushes in his grey trousers and green jumper. That green jumper, when you wash it, will smell of old man.

Again you wonder if you hate him. Think: has he stolen my life?

You wish things were different, that everything was different.

And you'll remember that particular afternoon – the one in the autumn, when you stood at your sink with a half peeled potato in your wet hands, and you watched him tend the rosebushes, when you hated him, when you made that wish – because that was the week before he died.

You'll remember his jumper too, the green woollen one, because that's what he was wearing and it still has his smell.

You are in your chair now. It's still morning and the house is quiet. You put his jumper to your nose, you breathe in slowly and again you wonder where he went.

Now tell me, how does that feel?

Sobs

I didn't take much notice of what the B & B looked like; after a long train ride and a shit couple of months I just wanted to lie down, be on my own, recover, you know? The owner, who checked me in, was an unremarkable man and I suspected both that he'd inherited the place and that he'd rather he hadn't. Not that he wasn't friendly or efficient – I guess I could just see through his smile, sense a shade of regret in his voice as he told me how great their breakfasts were.

I dumped my bag by the dressing table and did not look through the folder on its top marked, in black lettering on yellow card: Things To Do. I boiled the kettle, made myself a strong cup of tea, clay coloured, and drank it, lying on the bed. I liked the bed, its duvet was thin and the cover and pillowcases were floral and faded – but this was a bed I hadn't shared with Lynda. This was new, fresh, a sort of a beginning. So I lay there, even after I'd finished my tea. I closed my eyes, wanting to get some rest, some peace, before I needed to start thinking about where I'd go for dinner. And I fell asleep.

The first thing I was aware of when I was woken was the smell; not unpleasant, but heavy, musty, like the air had not been disturbed in some time, and I was surprised that I'd not noticed it earlier. The second thing was the crying. My first reaction was to frown and curse it; I'd heard enough crying and seen enough tears from Lynda over the past few months to last me a lifetime. I let my eyes get used to being open again, waited for things to become clear and then I sat up.

The crying was coming from behind me, from the room next to mine. And it belonged to a woman. I could tell that it had been happening for some time. You see, when a woman – well, any woman I've ever known – starts to cry it's loud and breathless and all over the place. Erratic. But this was quieter, gentler, it had a rhythm. This sounded like a lingering sadness. This was not the reaction to receiving some sudden and dreadful news.

I stood and walked into the bathroom, happy that the extractor fan was all I could hear. I took a shit and then showered.

I dried myself in the bathroom, relieved that the mirror had steamed over so that I couldn't see how fucking old I looked, and then I went back into the room, dragged my bag across the floor and sat on the end of the bed. The sobbing was still there, just as it had been before, slow, rhythmic and painfully sad. I ignored it as best as I could, concentrated on getting dressed, pulled on a pair of creased jeans and my good shirt. And still the sobs came. I stood, did my hair, squirted on the aftershave Lynda had bought me for Christmas – winced at that, winced because she was still around me like some spectre. And then I cursed that I had no-one with me to tell me I looked okay, nobody to lean towards me and make a slight adjustment to my fringe, close enough for me to taste her breath. I shook my head and sighed, picked up the Things To Do folder and sat back down on the bed.

But those sobs were still coming. There was nothing else; no voices, no arguing, no angry footsteps storming about the room. Just sobs. You know – I don't think she'd moved the whole time I'd been listening to her. So I guessed she must have been on her own.

I turned, I got to my knees on the bed, and crawled towards the wall. I put my hands on the pillows and listened. Just listened. To the sobs, to the girl. I put my ear to the wall, pressed it against the cold paint. And now I was closer, now I could hear more, the better I felt I understood things, suddenly it all made sense: it was like she was reading my soul. Like she was reading my sadness aloud. I thought: Shit! We're the same – and I wanted to reach through the wall right then and pull her close to my chest, kiss her head, stroke her hair, tell her it was all going to be all right. I wanted to soothe her, like I'd done all those times with Lynda.

But I didn't know it was all going to be all right, did I?

I sighed. My ear, the one against the wall, was warm now, and I could hear more than just sobs. I could hear the bed she was sitting on creaking in time with her, and I could hear the low gurgle – that sound of anguish, of despair – between her sobs. I could hear her breathe. I could hear her sniff. I could hear her sadness.

I wanted to make things better.

◆

I had considered mentioning the girl to the B & B's owner as I left for dinner, but I didn't. In the end I trusted my gut and kept it to myself. You see, I knew that pain, I understood what she was feeling, so if anyone was going to be able to help her it would be me. My gut also told me that she was beautiful. I imagined thick black curls and a smile I could kiss; shoulders that fitted my hands perfectly.

I ate a pie in a small pub where the locals didn't seem to like, or be used to, tourists, and while they gawped and talked about me I thought about fate. I considered serendipity. I wondered if this was all part of the plan

– were Lynda and I doomed before we'd even met? Our break-up, was it inevitable? Was this – the summer being shit, the bad weather, Lynda leaving me – was this all part of the plan to get me here, to meet this girl? And was the reason the girl in the room was so upset, was that all for me too? For us?

When the girl came to take my plates I said, Yes, I'd love another beer. It was helping me think. I drummed on the table's top with my fingers, it was newly wiped so it smelled sour, and while I wondered I finished my beer.

◆

I hoped that the owner wouldn't be around when I got back, and that I'd be able to look through the reservations list in his absence; knowing her name would be useful. He wasn't. But the counter, dimly lit by a single lamp, was bare except for a phone.

Back in my room I hung my coat on the hook behind the door and checked myself in the bathroom mirror. I adjusted my hair and then I cleaned my teeth. I looked better for having a beer I thought; there was some colour to my face and my skin looked smoother. I looked like a younger, happier man.

I climbed back onto the bed to listen for the girl, excited and feeling the beginnings of an erection.

But there was nothing. There were the dull sounds of conversations and movement elsewhere in the building and the faintest of hums from the lights. But no crying. No girl.

There was just me. Again. Alone, again. I felt as hollow as a cave and robbed. This girl, this crying girl, was supposed to be mine. This was supposed to be the beginning of my happily ever after. This was supposed to be my time for fuck's sake.

And that's when my tears came. When my sobs came, like puke, from my stomach. Uncontrollable and surging. Like explosions.

But after my tears came, so did a knocking at the door. It was rhythmic and I thought it sounded kind of sad.

The Angel in The Car Park

Two old ladies were standing in front of me as I waited at a bus stop near a car park. It had snowed heavily and while I waited to see if the bus would arrive – there were rumours it had been cancelled – I listened to them. The first one, the one on the right, with hair as fine as thread jutting out from under a headscarf, said, 'Might not be able to buy my angel this year.'

'No,' her friend said. It was neither a question nor a statement.

'First time since I was nine, it'll be,' she said. 'My father gave me my first, as a present. Brought it back from a business trip. Said it'd watch over me, keep me safe, just like he did.'

'Really,' said the lady's friend.

'It was beautiful. Made of china. No taller than my thumb. Lips as pink as a kitten's paws and oh how I loved it. Loved that I had something that'd look out for me.'

I moved closer.

The lady continued. 'I had quite a collection – even before my father died.'

'Oh,' said her friend.

'Heart attack. I don't know what I was thinking, really. But it seemed that with him gone I needed a little more looking after. So I jumped on the bus and I went into town and I came home with another angel.'

'Really.'

'Really. And I've done it every year since. Never missed one.' She shuffled closer to her friend and said, 'And I always make a point of doing it on his anniversary.'

'Lovely idea,' said her friend.

I noticed then that people were beginning to drift away. One lad, a mobile phone to his ear, said 'bus has been cancelled,' as he walked past me.

'Cancelled,' said the lady's friend. 'Doesn't look like I'll be able to buy my chops. And you won't be able to get this year's angel.'

The lady said nothing. I think she shook her head slightly, though I can't be sure.

She walked then, slowly, to a corner of the car park where the snow was thick and untouched. She placed her bag on the ground and she lay down on her back. Nobody said a word. Everybody watched. The lady moved her arms, down then up, flapping.

When she'd finished she stood, collected her bag, and walked away, not looking back once at what she'd created. Not once. I suppose she didn't have to.

Number 14

1.

The woman's house was a rainbow of squares. Its walls were a patchwork of Post-it notes, all equally spaced, almost aligned. Her walls were covered.

Each note, each square of fuchsia, cornflower, scarlet, emerald or lemon, bore a message, and each message was addressed to the person who'd written it: the woman. The messages had been written in biro or marker, usually in black ink; black ink provided the best contrast, made the words stand out, made them louder.

The woman was in her kitchen: hair up, wearing a vest top and three-quarter length trousers. She was barefoot and warm. She'd finished a bowl of Greek yoghurt and banana. She ran her index finger around the bowl, collecting the thin film of yoghurt like a tiny snow plough. She put her finger in her mouth and sucked. She was happy.

She placed the bowl and the spoon in the sink, then looked at the note (yellow) by the toaster. She read what it told her, and then she looked at the one next to it (green) and smiled slightly.

She made coffee then, milky and sweet and she went outside to the front of her house. The house, from the outside, looked like every other house on that street; if people saw it they would not think of walls covered in Post-it notes, they would not have a clue.

The woman did not like what she could see from her gate. She saw a woman pushing a buggy, a line of houses, pavement, walls and bushes. Not friends. She would have liked to have seen friends. She went back inside, spilling coffee on the back of her hand as she hurriedly locked the door. The blue note by the light switch, the colour of her mother's eyes, told her to KEEP SAFE.

She walked back into the kitchen and let herself out through the back door. In the fields beyond her garden she saw sheep and lambs and grass. She sat in her garden, her shoulders resting against the stone wall, her backside on the ground and her legs stretched out in front of her, toes pointing to the sky. She drank her coffee in the sun, watched birds in the trees above her and spiders, hanging like spit, in the bushes.

She said to herself, as she picked off the small pieces of grit that had stuck to the skin of her feet: I think I'll go into town. The walk'll do me good.

She locked her back door, put her mug in the sink, with the bowl and the spoon, and then pulled on a short jacket. She slipped her feet into pumps that made her think about ballet, and then she left her home.

2.

She met a man in town. He seemed sweet and caring and had a warm and handsome face. She let him buy her coffee; she knew him so it was okay – he delivered her mail. He made her smile when he told her her: name, address and postcode, and he made her giggle when he called her Number 14.

'We see it all,' he told her. 'Number 58 likes his porn. 71 has a Shopping Channel addiction, and I think the woman who lives at Highgate House is an artist.'

The woman said nothing, she just sipped her coffee and watched his mouth, enjoyed the shapes it made as he spoke.

'And you,' he said, setting down his cappuccino and pressing his hands, flat, onto the glass tabletop, 'You like stationery.'

She told him, with lips that looked soft and French, 'It's so I don't forget.'

She reached into her pocket then and produced a pack of Post-it notes and a pencil.

'Here,' she said, 'Write your number on this, and your name.'

She wanted to ask for more, wanted to demand he wrote down everything. She wanted his address, his email, where he went to school, grades, brothers, sisters, friends and references. She wanted to know about his first time, whether he was slow or fast in bed, what he liked to eat and what he thought about before going to sleep. She wanted a poem written just for her.

There were plenty of Post-its there in that deck. He could fill them all if he used his imagination. But, when he slid the pack back to her, all he had written on the pale yellow square on the top was, 'Eddie Fertig,' and a phone number.

'Foreign name?' the woman asked him.

'German.'

So that was it. That was all she was getting. She was disappointed.

'So, are you going to give me yours?' asked Eddie Fertig eagerly.

'I'll call you,' he was told. Besides, she thought, you know where I live – and if you're not going to tell me what I want to know then that's probably enough.

She finished her coffee and left.

3.

The woman saw Eddie Fertig twice over the following two weeks, once when the parcel was too large to fit through her letterbox and another time when she had to sign for the delivery; she used the marker she already had in her hand, it was heavy and awkward on his clipboard. The woman refused to meet his eye, and as soon as he'd gone she returned to her notes.

4.

She was making coffee when she decided to give him another chance. He seemed sweet. She was returning the milk to the fridge and as the door swished closed she noticed a note she'd stuck to it a while ago, the pencil words on its lemon background told her a name and a telephone number. She moved over to a drawer and pulled out a fresh pack of Post-its. She wrote neatly and slow, imagining she was writing on his back.

'Mr Eddie Fertig,' she began, black on pink. And when she'd finished she smiled and pulled the thin paper away from the pack, sticking it to her little finger. Then she began a second note.

5.

Eddie Fertig pulled a face when he read what was written on the pink note stuck above the letterbox on Number 14's door.

'Please come in?' he read aloud, talking to no-one but himself, 'Sure.'

The door was open. He stepped inside and took off his shoes as instructed, laying his mailbag next to them in the hall. Then he walked into the kitchen, where he found her, in a baby blue robe, soft and furry. She was leaning against the worktop. She shushed him and pointed to the table.

Eddie Fertig did as he was told. A mug waited for him there and the note stuck to it said, 'Eddie Fertig. Two sugars – I remember, see?' As he lifted it he noticed that it had been resting on another note, but the writing on that was obscured slightly by the faint outline of a ring.

'Well?' asked the woman.

Eddie Fertig read it and then nodded. 'Sure I still like you,' he said.

She smiled and adjusted her position. It looked like she was preparing herself, breathing in.

She pulled her robe open. There was a note stuck to her skin, it was sellotaped to her at one corner. Eddie had to move closer to read it; it hung between her naval and her breasts.

It said, 'If you want me, I'm yours.'

The yellow of the note intensified the colour of her skin, made it richer, browner, and made her hair look fierce and black.

Of course he wanted her.

6.

The woman cried that morning. She cried hard and she cried deep. She'd been prepared to – she'd wanted to give him a chance, to see if her body could be opened again. And it wasn't as though he'd been unreasonable.

'I like you, Number 14,' he'd said, 'very much. But I have one question.'

She should have known, should have seen it coming.

'What's with the walls?' he'd said. 'What's the deal with all these notes?'

'They're so I don't forget,' she'd told him.

'Then why's the same thing written on all of them? And who is Enoch anyway? Why "Enoch" over and over?'

The woman took Eddie Fertig's mug from him and placed it in the sink. She thanked him for the mail and then showed him out.

She closed the front door and locked it then ran back to the kitchen, collapsing – crying and half naked – on the floor. She cried hard and she cried deep, thinking of Enoch, knowing she could never forget him but knowing, also, that she was almost ready to try again.

So she stood, after some time, and moved to the sink where she cleaned the residue of tears from her face. She made herself coffee, fresh and milky and sweet, and she walked out into her garden to look at the birds and the grass and the sheep.

"News had just come over, we had five years left to cry in.
News guy wept and told us Earth was really dying"
– from the song *Five Years* by David Bowie.

Five Years and The Last Night on Earth

You spilled some when you put down your glass. I guess, somehow, or in some way, we all did. For you it was the way you put it down on the table, clumsy and awkward and abrupt, and it was the same for us I think; something spilled over, something dripped over our sides.

I can't blame you. Can't blame us. It was big news. A big shock. All of us lost something that day.

The news presenter was crying and I think that was the final straw, that's what made the man behind the counter, who minutes earlier had smiled as he'd served us – as he'd handed us milkshakes and ice-creams – turn off the TV. It left the place in silence. Nobody sipped. Nobody ate. Nobody spoke. Spoons were suspended and still, just like the open mouths of those who held them. The room, for a time, was frozen. It was like we were all in a photograph.

You took your hand from your glass and I opened mine and we touched, fingers to palm. It was as though we'd completed a circuit because that's when the room warmed, when people thawed, when we all came back to life. Once more there was noise. A growing rumble of chatter. Scared and desperate, some of it, and nervous and manic as well.

You said, 'Well, at least we have a date.'

And I said, 'Shit. I mean. Woah.'

You smiled at me and you said, 'Let's not waste a moment.'

And I was slow to respond, slow to think. My brain, sat there inside a warm skull, felt as frozen as your ice-cream.

You smiled at me again. I thought then how those pink lips would be the last thing I'd think of when our sun went out. Soft and pink and full of hope – I wouldn't have chosen anything else.

I remember telling you that. Remember saying, 'I hope the real thing's still with me.' And you promised it would be, that you would be. I said, 'And I could get one last kiss then?' and you nodded and told me, 'Yes'.

The girl at the table by the counter started freaking out, do you remember that? She was crying at first and then she fell to the floor, her stool clattering after her, and she beat it, she pummelled the tiles. So we left.

And then we were out in the street, your hand in my hand, or my hand in yours. Not that it matters, we were together – and happy, I guess, there in the street, the rain showering us, the wind sneaking inside our coats.

You said, 'So what are we going to do?'

And I said, 'Anything you want.'

We wrote a list that night, do you remember that? In bed, the duvet around us – promised each other we'd do as much of it as we could. Promised to enjoy the last five years together, promised to make the most of the last five years of Earth.

And, you know, it doesn't matter that we didn't get to do most of those things. Really, I'm not pissed off about that, I'm not angry. I just wish life hadn't become much crueller so suddenly, God knows things were difficult and short enough as they were.

I just wish you'd had the full five years.

And Gilly, I'm not even sure why I'm writing this. You'd think there must be more exciting ways to spend the last night on Earth. But this brings me closer to you. Gives me more than the image of your pink, smiling lips. And it gives me the chance to see your name and that helps me to see you, in a way.

And I can't think of a better way for all this to end than me looking at you.

I've just seen the clock. It's almost time, Gilly.

My Gilly.

I will watch you all the way to the end.

All the way.

To the end.

The End.

A number of the stories in this collection were published in the following literary magazines:

When You're Frightened, Honey, Think of Strawberries published in Ink, Sweat and Tears.

Seconds Are Ticking By published in SmokeLong Quarterly.

Pacifier published in Metazen.

Watching, Listening published in 3:AM Magazine.

Two Old Women Birdwatching in my Garden published in Metazen.

Pieces of Us published in The Pygmy Giant.

Say My Name published in Word Riot.

The Angel in the Car Park published in Rainy City Stories.

Number 14 published in Tomlit Quarterly.

Nik Perring lives in Cheshire where he writes, mostly, short stories. He's been writing things since 2003, first contributing to magazines and newspapers before moving on to fiction. His first book, one for children, was published in 2006.

Nik's real love is short stories and his have been published widely, online and in print, in the UK and abroad, appearing in 3:AM, SmokeLong Quarterly, Word Riot and Metazen, amongst others. His stories have been read at events, been printed on fliers, and used as part of an educational creative writing course.

Not So Perfect is his first collection.

http://nikperring.blogspot.com
www.nperring.com

Acknowledgements

I would like to thank the brilliant Faye Dayan for believing in my work and for sharing a vision of what this book could be. I should thank her too for being a dream to work with.

For their friendship, support and advice, I'd like to thank the wonderful Caroline Smailes, Tania Hershman and Anne Brooke.

For inspiration and for opening my eyes to what's possible to do with the short form I have to thank Aimee Bender, Etgar Keret and Sarah Salway; if I'd not read their work I would not have written this.

Thanks also to Mum and Dad and to all my family and friends (on-line and off, you know who you are) who've helped, encouraged, put up with, and supported me, including Barge Bob and, from afar, Gary Hall.

Thanks to all those who've published my work over the last few years, especially SmokeLong Quarterly, 3:AM, Rainy City Stories, Tomlit Quarterly, Metazen, Ink Sweat and Tears, Word Riot and The Pygmy Giant.

And thank you: Michael Kimball, Michael Czyzniejewski, Joe Melia, Susan Tomaselli and Vanessa Gebbie for your kind words and wonderful support.